The Adventure of the Backyard Sleep-out

The Adventure of the Backyard Sleep-out

by Nancy McArthur

illustrated by
Irene Trivas

A
LITTLE·APPLE
PAPERBACK

SCHOLASTIC INC.
New York Toronto London Auckland Sydney

No part of this publication may be reproduced in whole or in part, or stored in a retrieval system, or transmitted in any form or by any means, electronic, mechanical, photocopying, recording, or otherwise, without written permission of the publisher. For information regarding permission, write to Scholastic Inc., 730 Broadway, New York, NY 10003.

ISBN 0-590-45033-6

12 11 10 9 8 7 6 5 4 3 2 1   2 3 4 5 6 7/9

Printed in the U.S.A.   28

First Scholastic printing, April 1992

For Daniel McArthur

The Adventure of
the Backyard Sleep-out

Chapter 1

Susie sometimes grumbled about having to take her dog, Puddles, for walks. But once they were on their way, she liked doing it.

She waved to neighbors and stopped to talk to people she knew. Pud tugged on the leash to keep her going. Often Pud would stop to smell the scents left by other animals. Then Susie tugged on the leash to keep *him* going.

This Saturday morning, the first person they met was Tim. He stopped his bike to tell Susie some news.

Pud sniffed at the bike's back tire. He smelled a strange dog. Nosing at the edge of the sidewalk, he found a whiff of rabbits. He wanted to follow this trail, so he pulled hard on the leash. But Susie did not budge.

Tim said, "Eric got a tent for his birthday!"

"Is he going camping?" asked Susie.

"Not till his dad gets back from a business trip in two weeks," Tim said. "But they set it up in their backyard. I'm going over to see it right now."

"I want to see, too," said Susie. Tim rode slowly so she and Pud could keep up.

The tent was yellow with rounded sides. Eric stuck his head out when he heard them. "Come in," he said.

Susie told Pud, "Sit!" He flopped on the grass and rolled over.

She thought the tent was small inside, but she didn't say so. "This would make a good clubhouse," she said, "for a club that only has three members."

Eric explained, "For camping, it's a two-people tent."

They sat down cross-legged.

Susie said, "Let's pretend we're out in the woods."

"Okay," agreed Eric.

She said, "We just came back from a hike."

"I'm hungry from all that walking," said Tim.

"We already ate on the hike," Susie said.

Tim said, "Now it's night. It's really dark out. Owls are hooting. Hoot-hoot! Bears and wolves are sneaking around out-side." He growled. Then he looked very

serious. "I think I hear something," he said.

Through the tent flap poked Pud's fuzzy face.

"It's a bear!" shouted Eric, laughing.

"Hello, bear," said Susie. "Come in and camp out with us." Pud squeezed into the tent and licked her nose.

They all laughed.

"The bear thinks you taste good," said Eric.

"Be careful," said Tim, smiling. "Don't let him eat you up."

Susie chuckled. "He already ate on the hike," she said. "Now I have to walk him home before he gets hungry again."

She pushed Pud out of the tent and crawled out after him.

She told Eric, "It's too bad you have to wait two weeks to go camping."

He replied, "I get to keep the tent up in the yard until we go. And my mom said

I could stay out here tonight with a friend." He told Tim, "That's you."

"Great!" exclaimed Tim.

Susie and Pud went on their way. The boys started planning what they would need for their camp-out.

"Peanut butter sandwiches," said Eric. "Two apiece."

Tim asked, "Do pizza places deliver to tents?"

Chapter 2

Back home Susie put food and water in Pud's dishes. Feeding him was her job.

While he slurped loudly, she went next door to Megan's.

Megan and Annie were sitting on the dining room floor. They were playing with the dollhouse Megan had made from a cardboard box.

Megan was cutting a piece of cardboard to glue on top of a spool of thread to make a table.

Her mother and grandmother were unfolding a huge tablecloth. When they put it on the table, the sides came down to the floor.

"This is much too big," said Megan's mother. "I'll have to take it back to the store and get a smaller size." The women went into the kitchen.

Susie told her friends about the boys camping out.

"Are they ever lucky!" said Annie.

"Did you ever go camping?" asked Susie.

"No," replied Annie.

Megan said, "My brother did once and he liked it. Even though it rained and the tent leaked and his sleeping bag got wet and the food was terrible and he got lots of mosquito bites and fell in a river."

"Maybe that will happen to Eric and Tim," said Susie.

"Eric doesn't have a river in his yard," said Annie.

"Then," said Megan, "they won't have as much fun as Mike did."

"I wish we could camp out in the yard, too," said Susie.

"Let's do it," said Megan.

Megan's big orange cat, Fluffo, slid his head out from under the tablecloth to sneak up on the spool. He liked anything that rolled.

He loved to knock pencils off tables so he could bat them around the floor. But spools were better. He waited patiently.

"We don't have a tent," said Annie. "Does your brother have one?"

"Nope. It was somebody else's tent," said Megan. "He borrowed the sleeping bag, too."

A big furry paw darted out and swiped the spool.

Megan grabbed, but Fluffo was too fast for her.

To get at him, she had to crawl under the table.

With the tablecloth hanging down on all sides, it seemed like a tent under there.

"Hey, come in here," she said.

Annie and Susie crawled in. Fluffo had to move over. It was getting crowded.

"When I was little," Megan said, "I used to play hideout under here. Maybe we could camp out here."

"That would be camping in, not out," said Susie.

Megan grinned. "Let's take the table out in the yard."

Susie liked that idea. "We could have a picnic on top of it and sleep under it. Everybody would say, 'What is that dining room table doing out in the yard all night?' "

"Fluffo can come with us," said Megan, "in case there are any spools to attack."

They heard footsteps. Megan's grandmother said, "I hear you talking, but I don't see you. You must be invisible."

They giggled.

"Aha!" said Grandma. "Invisible gigglers! I knew Fluffo could disappear fast. I didn't know you could do it, too." She peeked under the tablecloth. "It's nice under there, isn't it?" she said. "I used to play under tables when I was a girl. It's like being in a cave."

"We want to camp out in the backyard," said Megan, "but we don't have a tent. So we're pretending this is one."

"My friends and I used to make our own tent," said Grandma. "We put a blanket over a clothesline."

"We could use this tablecloth," said Megan. "It's really big."

"No," said Grandma. "I'll find you an old blanket."

"We don't have a clothesline, either," said Annie.

"What's a clothesline?" asked Susie.

12

"That's what you hang clothes on in the backyard," Annie said.

"Why would you do that?" asked Susie.

Grandma explained, "Before dryers were invented, everybody hung their washed clothes outside to dry in good weather. Lots of people still do that."

"But not their underwear," said Megan.

"Yes, that too," said Grandma.

"Oooh," said Megan, making a horrible face. "I wouldn't want anybody to see my underwear hanging outside."

"Nobody cared," said Grandma. "Everybody's underwear was hanging outside."

"I'm glad we have a dryer," said Megan.

"So am I," replied Grandma. "It makes things a lot easier. But clothes smell so good when they dry in the sunshine."

Chapter 3

Later Grandma brought over some white rope and an old brown-and-white cotton blanket.

Susie's backyard had the two trees they needed. Grandma tied the rope between them so it sagged low in the middle. She put the blanket over it. The edges dragged on the ground.

Susie did not see how a blanket on a rope was going to be a tent.

"Everybody take a corner," Grandma told them. She showed them how to pull the blanket open to make a big upside-down V.

It looked like an old-fashioned tent Susie had seen a picture of in a book.

Grandma said, "Now find four rocks or something else heavy to hold the corners down to keep it open."

All they could find were little stones that wouldn't hold anything down.

Megan went to look in her garage. The first heavy thing she found was Fluffo. He was busy snoozing. He opened one eye to see what was happening and closed it again.

"Would you like to come sleep on a corner of our tent?" asked Megan.

He gave a big contented sigh and snoozed on.

The only other heavy thing she found that she could carry was a leftover can of paint. She lugged it over to Susie's.

Eric and Tim were there.

"What is this old blanket hanging here for?" asked Tim.

"It's going to be a tent," said Susie. "We're camping out tonight, too."

"Are you kidding?" asked Eric.

"What are you going to do with that paint?" asked Tim.

"You'll see," said Megan.

The boys sat down on the grass to watch.

"Not now," she said. "You have to come back later."

"What time?" asked Tim.

"After dinner."

As the boys went away, Eric said, "Maybe it's a joke. Maybe Megan's going to paint the word *tent* on that blanket."

Susie said, "Our tent isn't going to be as good as theirs."

"I don't care," said Megan. "It's better than no tent at all."

Susie said, "Then if they don't like it, that's tough noogies!"

16

Annie came back from her house with a heavy bookend that looked like an eagle. She went back to get the other one.

"Now we need one more heavy thing," said Susie.

"I know!" said Megan. She ran into her house. She came back with a five-pound bag of cat litter.

They spread out the tent sides and put the heavy things on the corners. They sat down inside.

"This is great!" said Susie.

Megan stretched out to see what it was going to be like to sleep there. Susie and Annie lay down, too.

"Move over a little," said Susie. "We need room for Pud. He always sleeps in my room."

"This isn't your room," said Megan.

"We should have a watchdog," said Annie.

Megan joked, "I'll bring my watchcat."

Chapter 4

After dinner the girls each brought two blankets, a pillow, a flashlight, and lots of snacks. They folded the blankets longways to sleep on.

Susie also brought some books. Annie brought her favorite stuffed animal, a pink rabbit called Bunnywunny.

They lay down on their blanket beds to try them out. Megan's elbow hit Susie in the ribs. Annie's foot bumped Megan's head.

"Lie down the other way," said Megan. "I don't want your feet in my face."

"You turn around," said Annie. "I was here first."

"There's no room for Pud," said Susie. "He'll have to sleep outside the tent."

"What if we have to go to the bathroom?" asked Annie.

"We can go in the house for that," said Susie. "If we want a drink of water, we can use the hose."

The boys came over.

"This is a different kind of tent," said Eric.

"Are you really going to sleep here?" asked Tim.

"Sure," said Megan. "We're going to eat snacks and read books with our flashlights and stay up very, very late."

Annie added, "We have a watchdog and a watchbunny."

Susie said, "I bet we stay up later than you do."

Eric asked, "Do you want to see what we've got in our tent?"

They all went over to his yard. The boys had comfy sleeping bags on top of a soft rug. They had a big battery lantern that could light up the whole tent. There was a stack of plastic boxes.

"Snacks," explained Tim. "In plastic boxes so bugs can't get at them."

On the way back, Annie said, "I didn't think about bugs. Do you think some will come in our tent?"

"If they do," said Megan, "we can squash them."

Chapter 5

The girls got an old throw rug from Susie's mother. They sat on it outside their tent, waiting for the sky to get dark. That seemed to be taking an awfully long time.

They decided to be cowgirls for a while. They galloped around the yard. Pud galloped with them.

Megan's grandmother came over and took pictures of them with their tent.

Annie's parents brought some more snacks. Her father told them, "I checked the weather report. It's not going to rain."

Mike came out to see their tent. "Watch out for killer mosquitoes," he warned. "And animals that prowl in the woods at night."

"This is not the woods," said Annie.

"Never mind him," said Megan. "He likes to say stuff like that."

Susie's mother said, "Be sure to come in if you need anything. Or if you decide not to stay out all night. I'm leaving the back door unlocked and a light on."

Their neighbor on the other side, Mrs. Johnson, came over to see what they were doing. "This is a wonderful tent," she said. She brought them some more snacks.

Susie's father clipped Pud's leash to his collar. He snapped the loop on the other end around the clothesline. "This will let Pud walk if he wants to, but not far," he said.

"Why is it taking so long to get dark?" asked Susie.

"It just seems that way," said her father. "Go put on your pajamas and brush your teeth. Then you'll be all set."

They put on their pajamas and robes in Susie's room. They decided to brush their teeth outside with water from the hose.

Without a sink, they had to spit out the foamed-up toothpaste on the grass.

"Yuck," said Annie, looking down at the little white gobs of goo.

"We're really camping out now," said Megan.

They ate snacks for a while. Then Annie said they should brush their teeth again. So they did. They spit more little gobs of goo on the grass. Then they ate more snacks and brushed again.

It was getting darker. They crawled into their tent and read books for a while. Their flashlights made little circles of light. They did not light up the whole tent like Eric and Tim's lantern.

Birds twittered in the trees. After a while they stopped.

"They've gone to sleep," said Megan.

The outside of Susie's house looked different in the dark. They could see parts of rooms through the lighted windows.

It was not completely dark. There was light up high from the streetlights in front of the house.

A far-off dog barked. Cars drove by. Someone called a dog. A back door slammed. From an open window in a house nearby they could hear a TV going.

Near the tent, a cricket chirped in the grass. A breeze made the trees and bushes rustle.

"There's a lot more noise out here than inside," said Annie.

"I wonder what Tim and Eric are doing," said Susie.

"Let's go spy on them," said Megan. "Maybe we can scare them."

Annie said, "We can't go down the street in our pajamas and bathrobes."

"Let's sneak through the backyards,"

said Susie. "If we hurry, we'll be back before my mom and dad find out we're gone."

"We shouldn't do this," said Annie. They crossed the driveway toward Mrs. Johnson's backyard.

They heard a window go up. "Hold it right there!" Susie's mom called. "Where do you three think you're going?"

"Nowhere," said Susie. That was true because now they couldn't go.

"Back in the yard!" said her mom. "And stay put!"

She watched until they got back in the tent.

Chapter 6

Fluffo slept on Megan's bed at night, but she was not there. He waited for a while. Then he trotted downstairs to hunt for her. She was not in the house.

Mike was at the kitchen table eating a piece of chicken.

"Hi, Mr. Fluffaduff," said Mike. He rubbed Fluffo's ribs gently with his foot.

But a rib rub was not what Fluffo wanted. He sat down and tilted his head at Mike. That didn't work, so he leaped up on the table. Mike put him back on the floor.

Fluffo rubbed against Mike's leg. Nothing happened. So he gently sank his claws in. Mike's fingers came down with a piece of chicken.

Before Fluffo had a chance to pester Mike for another piece, he saw Megan's mother's shoes go by toward the back door.

"I'm going to check on the girls," she said, holding the door open. Fluffo sped past her into the night.

Megan's mother and the girls went around calling Fluffo. But he never came when called unless he felt like it. Right now he felt like sitting in the bushes and watching them run around. He could see very well in dark places.

Of course, Pud smelled where the cat was. But as long as it did not bother him, he would not bother it.

After they gave up trying to find Fluffo, the girls settled down, just talking, in the tent.

Pud heard somebody coming. He did not bark.

The girls heard the bushes rustle. They didn't know it wasn't a breeze.

Suddenly they heard loud growling. Pud growled back.

The girls shot out of the tent and ran for the back door. Behind them, they heard loud laughing.

Eric and Tim were standing by the tent.

"You rats!" exclaimed Susie.

"Yeah!" said Annie.

A window went up. "Everybody back to your tents!" ordered Susie's mom. "Right this minute! Or I'm calling all your mothers!"

The boys went back through the bushes, still laughing.

The girls crawled back into their tent.

"Pud's supposed to be our watchdog," said Annie. "Why didn't he bark?"

"Because he likes them," said Susie.

The downstairs lights in her house went out, except the one by the back door. Soon a light went on upstairs in the bathroom.

Susie said, "My mom likes to soak in the tub. If we go right now, we can get back before she looks out again."

They were three backyards down the block before Annie whispered, "We shouldn't be doing this."

They often went through backyards in the daytime. But everything looked different in the dark. Susie led the way with her flashlight. She pushed a bush branch out of their way. But it slipped from her hand and whapped Megan in the face.

At Eric's they peeked around the side

of the garage. The yellow tent glowed with light. The boys' shadows on the sides were very big. Music played softly, but loud enough to keep Eric and Tim from hearing the girls.

Megan whispered, "Who's good at growling noises?"

"Not me," said Annie.

"Me, neither," added Susie. "But if we do growling, they'll know it's us. We need something better." Then she remembered something she had seen in Eric's front yard that morning.

"See that hose hooked up on the side of the house?" she whispered. "There's a sprinkler on the end of it."

Susie led the way. They circled around the house next door to get to the front yard. Susie grabbed the sprinkler and carried it with the hose dragging behind. They stopped by the back corner of the house.

Susie took a deep breath. Tiptoeing as

fast as she could, she put the sprinkler near the side of the tent.

Annie and Megan held their breath while they watched.

Susie scurried back and turned on the faucet.

Water spurted from the sprinkler, but not at the tent.

"It's squirting the wrong way," whispered Megan.

"Just wait," said Susie. "It's the kind that goes back and forth."

"We'd better go back," said Annie.

"No," said Megan, "I want to see this."

Slowly the sprinkler began to move. Soon the water sprayed straight up in the air. Slowly it moved over to the other side. At last it pattered loudly on the tent.

The shadows jumped.

Eric said, "It's not supposed to rain."

"It's sort of nice to hear rain on the roof," said Tim. The sprinkler started moving back the other way.

36

"It's stopped," said Eric. "That's the fastest rainstorm there ever was."

The girls pressed their hands over their mouths to keep from laughing out loud.

Soon the sprinkler hit the tent again.

"Here it comes again," said Eric.

"And there it goes again," said Tim.

The rain pattered and stopped once more.

Eric said, "That's a funny kind of rain." He came out of the tent. "The grass is wet, but it's not raining now," he said. Tim came out, too.

"Do you hear something that sounds a little like rain?" asked Tim. They turned toward the sound just as the sprinkler moved back and sprinkled all over them.

The boys heard giggling going away through the bushes.

"It's them!" said Eric. "It sounds like they're going the long way around through the yards. If we take our bikes, we can beat them back to Susie's."

"But what can we do when we get there?" asked Tim.

"Bring that big snacks box," said Eric.

They rode down the street barefooted in their pajamas.

Chapter 7

Susie had dropped her flashlight behind Eric's garage. On the way back they had to go more slowly.

Bush branches kept swatting them. Something grabbed Megan's sleeve. "Yikes!" she said loudly.

She heard a little rip. "Thorns," she said. "Be careful."

Fluffo crept silently along behind the girls. He kept stopping to look at interesting things like bugs. He pounced at a mouse, but it got away. Then he ran ahead of the girls and waited for them. They were not as good at sneaking as he was.

Reaching Susie's backyard, they were glad to see the bathroom light was still on. Then they saw the boys scramble out of the tent.

As they ran for their bikes, Tim said, "Ugh! I stepped in something slimy."

"Toothpaste," said Susie, chuckling.

Everything in their tent looked just the way they left it.

"They didn't do anything," said Annie.

"We scared them away before they got a chance to," said Megan.

"What snacks are left?" asked Susie. They passed the food around.

Annie put some carrot sticks next to her pink rabbit. "Bunnywunny loves carrots," she said, laughing.

A window went up. Susie's mom called from the bathroom, "Is everything all right out there?"

"Yes," called Susie.

Her mother said, "Settle down now and go to sleep. It's long past your bedtime." The window closed. The light went out.

Even with the streetlights, the neighborhood was much darker now.

Megan put her flashlight down so it made a little circle of light on the inside of the tent.

"For a night-light," she explained.

"You'll wear out your batteries," warned Annie.

"I don't care," said Megan.

Annie was the first to crawl into her blanket bed. "Bugs!" she exclaimed and crawled right out again. She grabbed Megan's flashlight to look between the blankets.

"Crackers!" she said.

Megan and Susie found crunched-up

crackers in their beds, too.

They had to unfold all their blankets and shake them out on the grass. Then they folded them up again.

"What a mess," said Annie. "Let's go over there and do something else to them."

"It's getting too late," said Susie. "Besides, we already got Tim with the gobs of toothpaste goo."

They settled down in their blankets. They all lay down the same way, so nobody would get feet in the face. Susie lay across one end with Pud next to her right outside on the rug. Megan was in the middle. Annie, at the other end, put her pink rabbit on the outside edge. "Bunny-wunny can guard us on this side," she said.

They talked quietly for a while. Soon the spaces between talking got longer and longer.

Then when Susie asked a question, nobody answered. "Megan?" she said. "Annie?" She reached out and patted Pud. "We're the only ones awake," she told him. But he did not move. He was asleep, too.

Chapter 8

For a long time Susie tried to go to sleep. But this was not like being in her own bed in her own room.

Bushes rustled. Tree branches creaked spookily.

Suddenly something moved at the far end of the tent. Her heart went thud. Then she saw it was only Fluffo creeping in. He snuggled up next to Megan.

With three in the tent, there was little room to turn over. There was no room to spread out the way Susie liked to in her own bed. She hadn't known the ground could feel so hard, even through blankets.

Camping out was not as easy as she thought it would be.

Then Megan rolled over. Her arm flopped on top of Susie.

Susie did not like having somebody's arm on her. If she pushed it off, maybe Megan would wake up. Then Susie could ask her if she wanted to go sleep in the house. But then Annie would be left outside alone. If she woke up and they were gone, Annie would be afraid.

Maybe she could wiggle out from under Megan's arm and go in the house by herself. Then she could get up very early and come back out. They wouldn't know she chickened out.

But in case they woke up before she got back, she should leave them a note. She would have to go in the house to write it. Then she would come back and put it in front of Megan's flashlight.

First she had to get out from under Megan's arm.

Suddenly, from the other end of the tent she heard a loud MUNCH! She froze.

MUNCH-MUNCH-MUNCH went whatever was out there. It had to be an animal. She hoped it wasn't a big one. She slowly turned her head.

Past Megan and Fluffo and Annie she saw two rabbits. Only one was pink. The other was brown and eating a carrot stick.

Susie had to get out of there. She pushed Megan's arm over, bumping Fluffo. She crawled out of the tent, right over Pud.

The cat and dog woke up smelling rabbit.

Fluffo pounced at the brown rabbit but it took off. He landed on the pink one and sank his claws into it.

Pud galloped over Megan and Annie. That woke them up. The loop of his leash

dragged along the clothesline after him. It pushed the tent along the line.

He pulled so hard on the leash that the tent corners were yanked from under the paint can, bookends, and bag of cat litter.

"Where's the tent going?" asked Megan as it whisked away.

The tree at the end of the clothesline stopped the crumpled-up tent and Pud's leash, too.

Fluffo quickly lost interest in the pink rabbit because it did not move. He let Megan rescue it from his clutches without a fight.

Annie hugged her rabbit. "Poor Bunny-wunny!" she said. "Are you all right?"

Susie told them about the brown rabbit.

"Where did it go?" asked Megan.

"Pud and Fluffo chased it away," replied Susie.

"They saved us from a rabbit?" asked Annie.

"It was a pretty big one," said Susie.

"I'm going in to the bathroom. Does anybody want to come along?"

"Me," said Annie.

Megan said, "I'm not staying out here by myself!"

The yard was very dark, even with flashlights. The night felt damp and chilly now. Their tent was all squashed against a tree.

Susie asked, "Does anybody want to sleep in the house?"

"Yes!" said Megan.

Annie said, "Let's go!"

Fluffo was trying to wriggle out of Megan's arms.

Susie unsnapped Pud's leash from the line. She dragged him and her blankets toward the house. Annie piled everything else on one of her blankets and hauled it to the back door.

Chapter 9

Inside, Fluffo escaped from Megan. He dashed into the living room and crawled on his belly like an alligator under the couch.

Pud ran upstairs to his usual sleeping spot next to Susie's bed.

He waited a while, but Susie did not come. So he went downstairs to get her. He smelled the cat along with the girls, but he followed them into the living room anyway.

One light was on. The girls were asleep on the blankets on the soft carpet. From under the couch two yellow eyes glared at him.

He knew the cat would not come out while he was there. He stretched out next to Susie. Pud sighed happily and closed his eyes.

Soon, under the couch, Fluffo fell asleep, too.

Outside, in the dark, the brown rabbit hopped back into the yard and ate the rest of the carrot sticks.

When Megan's mother got up at 7 A.M., she looked out to check on the girls. She saw no tent and no girls, just eagle book-ends, a paint can, and a bag of cat litter.

She called Susie's house. Susie's father found them in the living room and told her they were all right.

She came over to see for herself. Soon Annie's parents were ringing the back doorbell. Then Mrs. Johnson came over to see what happened.

The girls woke up because of the loud laughing and talking in the kitchen.

The grown-ups were telling about how they camped out in the yard when they were kids.

Mrs. Johnson said, "It rained, and our tent leaked, so we had to go in."

Annie's mother said, "Every time I looked out of our tent, my mother was looking out the window at us. We couldn't sleep, so we went in. She said if we had stayed out all night, she would have watched out the window all night."

Megan's mother said, "My brother kept telling me creepy stories. He scared me silly. So I went in the house and left him out there alone. Then he got scared, so he came in, too."

Susie's father said, "My friends and I ran all over the neighborhood in our pajamas. We thought that was great."

"Don't let the girls hear you say that," said Susie's mother.

"Then the next day one of the neighbors told my father," he continued, "and we really got it."

Susie whispered to Annie and Megan, "Do you think anybody saw us?"

"I hope not," said Megan.

Annie's father said, "I couldn't sleep because the ground felt really hard. So I went inside. My bed never felt so good!"

Susie's mother asked, "Didn't anybody stay out all night?" Nobody said yes.

The girls went into the kitchen and got hugs. Susie fed Pud. Megan dragged Fluffo from under the couch. He left claw tracks on the rug. Her mother took him home to feed him.

The girls carried their bowls of cereal into the living room and ate on the floor. They pretended to make a camp fire and cook over it.

"Let's make hamburgers," said Susie. "Pud, would you like a hamburger?" She put out her hand with nothing in it.

Pud knew that word. He looked at her hand hopefully, but there was nothing there.

"Yum, yum," said Susie, munching on air. "I love hamburgers for breakfast when I'm camping out."

Chapter 10

Outside, Tim looked around to see what he had stepped in last night.

"This white stuff must be it," he told Eric.

Eric poked it carefully with one finger. "It's not slimy now," he said. "It's all dried out."

The girls came out with Pud.

"What happened to your tent?" asked Eric.

Susie told him.

"You should get a tent like mine," he said. "A dog couldn't knock that down."

"It could if you got a big enough dog," said Megan.

Susie said, "Ours didn't get knocked down exactly. It was more like sideways."

Annie wondered why the boys were not bragging about staying out all night. So she asked, "Did you stay out all night?"

"Almost," replied Eric. "My mom caught us coming back on our bikes. She made us go in the house."

"Eric has bunk beds," said Tim. "I got to sleep in the top one."

Susie bragged, "We camped out on the living room floor."

"That's not camping out," said Tim.

"Then it's camping in," she said. "Sleeping in bunk beds is not camping at all."

Tim asked, "What's that white stuff over there on the grass?"

"Toothpaste," said Megan. "We brushed our teeth outside and spit right there. We did it lots of times to make lots of goo gobs."

Tim scrunched up his face. "It's a good thing I wiped my foot off good," he said. "So I won't get toothpaste spit germs."

Megan said, "We don't have spit germs."

"Yes, we do," said Annie. "Everybody has them. That's why you're not supposed to use somebody else's toothbrush."

"Yeah," said Susie. "Dogs have spit germs, too. Every time Pud licks my fingers, I'm supposed to wash my hands before I touch any food."

"Then don't let him use your toothbrush," said Eric. They all started to laugh.

Tim headed for his bike. Eric followed.

"Where are you going?" asked Annie.

"Home to wash my foot!" said Tim, grinning. "With hot water! And soap, too!"

Laughing, the girls flopped down on the

grass. Pud ran around them and licked Susie's nose.

"Uh-oh," said Annie with a giggle. "Now you have to wash your nose before you touch any food with it!"

Megan said, "Let's make our tent again." They spread out the blanket along the line and put the heavy things on the corners.

They crawled in and sat cross-legged.

"This would be a good little clubhouse," said Susie.

"We could camp out here in the daytime," said Annie. "And eat lunch here."

"We can take turns camping in at night at all our houses," said Megan.

"But," said Susie, "let's go outside to brush our teeth!"

About the Author

Nancy McArthur grew up loving all kinds of books, and by age thirteen decided to become an author.

Ideas for Nancy's books can begin with one special phrase that comes to her mind. She writes the idea down quickly, and then starts adding other thoughts to it. Her stories unfold as she writes them. "You picture your characters in situations, and they just start doing things," she says.

Nancy revises her work and before finishing a book, she tests it on children, reading it aloud. "You watch their faces," she says, "and it tells you where to cut, what's funny, and what isn't clear."

Now, at age 59, Nancy McArthur says "that seems really old to you, but not to me." She is a teacher at Baldwin-Wallace College, as well as an author. Among her best-selling books are *The Adventure of the Buried Treasure*, *Megan Gets a Dollhouse*, and *Pickled Peppers*. She lives in Berea, Ohio.

LITTLE ![apple] APPLE ®

BABY·SITTERS

Little Sister ™

by Ann M. Martin, author of *The Baby-sitters Club* ®

❑	MQ44300-3	#1	Karen's Witch	$2.75
❑	MQ44259-7	#2	Karen's Roller Skates	$2.75
❑	MQ44299-6	#3	Karen's Worst Day	$2.75
❑	MQ44264-3	#4	Karen's Kittycat Club	$2.75
❑	MQ44258-9	#5	Karen's School Picture	$2.75
❑	MQ44298-8	#6	Karen's Little Sister	$2.75
❑	MQ44257-0	#7	Karen's Birthday	$2.75
❑	MQ42670-2	#8	Karen's Haircut	$2.75
❑	MQ43652-X	#9	Karen's Sleepover	$2.75
❑	MQ43651-1	#10	Karen's Grandmothers	$2.75
❑	MQ43650-3	#11	Karen's Prize	$2.75
❑	MQ43649-X	#12	Karen's Ghost	$2.75
❑	MQ43648-1	#13	Karen's Surprise	$2.75
❑	MQ43646-5	#14	Karen's New Year	$2.75
❑	MQ43645-7	#15	Karen's in Love	$2.75
❑	MQ43644-9	#16	Karen's Goldfish	$2.75
❑	MQ43643-0	#17	Karen's Brothers	$2.75
❑	MQ43642-2	#18	Karen's Home-Run	$2.75
❑	MQ43641-4	#19	Karen's Good-Bye	$2.75
❑	MQ44823-4	#20	Karen's Carnival	$2.75
❑	MQ44824-2	#21	Karen's New Teacher	$2.75
❑	MQ44833-1	#22	Karen's Little Witch	$2.75
❑	MQ44832-3	#23	Karen's Doll	$2.75
❑	MQ44859-5	#24	Karen's School Trip	$2.75
❑	MQ44831-5	#25	Karen's Pen Pal	$2.75
❑	MQ44830-7	#26	Karen's Ducklings	$2.75
❑	MQ44829-3	#27	Karen's Big Joke	$2.75
❑	MQ44828-5	#28	Karen's Tea Party	$2.75
❑	MQ44825-0	#29	Karen's Cartwheel	$2.75
❑	MQ43647-3		Karen's Wish Super Special #1	$2.95
❑	MQ44834-X		Karen's Plane Trip Super Special #2	$2.95
❑	MQ44827-7		Karen's Mystery Super Special #3	$2.95

Available wherever you buy books, or use this order form.